The Children Who Loved Books

Peter Carnavas

Kane Miller
A DIVISION OF EDC PUBLISHING

For Sophie and Elizabeth,
my favourite storytellers

Angus and Lucy didn't have very much.

They didn't have a television.

They didn't have a car.

They didn't even have a house.

But Angus and Lucy had books ...

hundreds of them.

They were stacked here

and piled there,

balanced, propped and shoved
in all kinds of odd places.

Books cluttered every corner of their home,

until one day ...

...their home could take no more.

The books had to go.

But things were not the same.

Bowls slid off the table.

Angus couldn't reach the window.

And because there was more space in their home,

there was a lot more space between them all.

Then one afternoon,
something tumbled from Lucy's school bag.

"What's this?" said Dad.
"A book," Lucy answered.
"From where?" asked Mom.
"The library," Lucy replied.

Mom and Dad looked at the book. They opened it.
Dad read the first sentence aloud, then the second.

The children moved closer
as Dad turned the page and read on.

The light faded, and the family moved inside,
Dad reading all the way.

They huddled beside the lamp
and listened to the story.

That night, as darkness fell upon the town,

one small home shone brighter than any other.

The next day, as the family yawned their good mornings,
they were closer than ever before.

With bleary eyes and full hearts,
they rode through the clean morning air.

Nobody had said a word, but
Angus and Lucy knew exactly where they were going.

Angus and Lucy didn't have very much,
but they had all they would ever need.